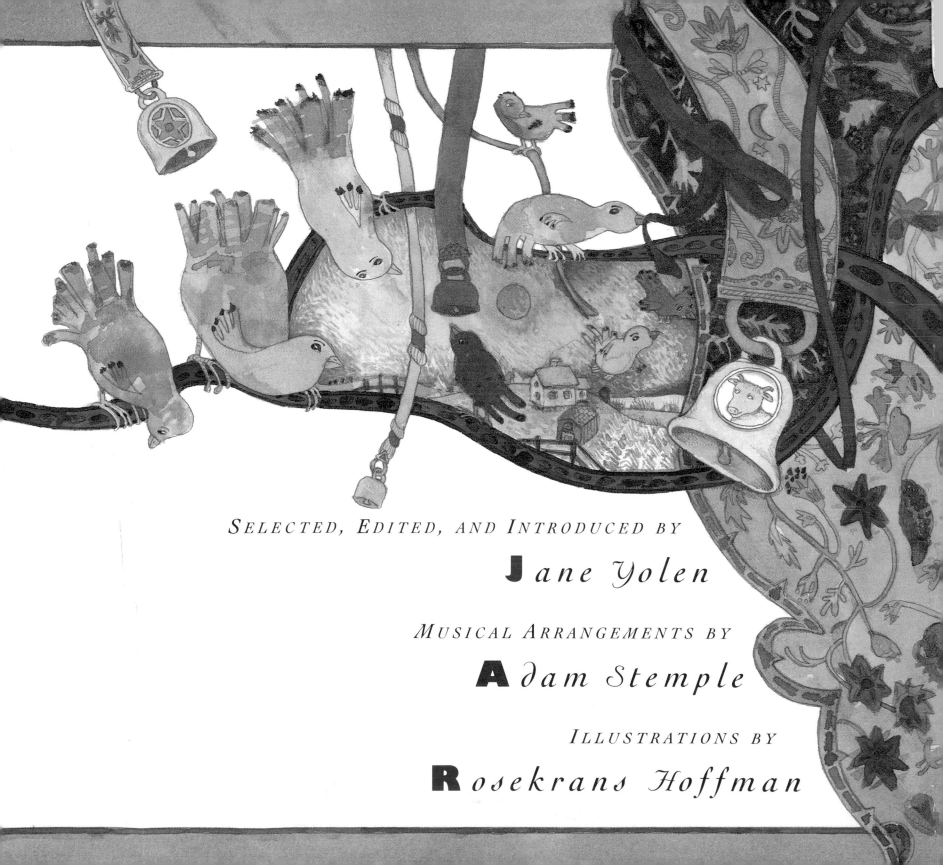

SELECTED, EDITED, AND INTRODUCED BY
Jane Yolen

MUSICAL ARRANGEMENTS BY
Adam Stemple

ILLUSTRATIONS BY
Rosekrans Hoffman

Jane Yolen's
Old MacDonald
Songbook

Jane Yolen's Old MacDonald Songbook

Boyds Mills Press

Text copyright © 1994 by Jane Yolen

Musical arrangements © 1994 by Adam Stemple

Illustrations copyright © 1994 by Rosekrans Hoffman

Published by Caroline House

Boyds Mills Press, Inc.

A Highlights Company

815 Church Street

Honesdale, Pennsylvania 18431

Printed in Mexico

Publisher Cataloging-in-Publication Data

Main entry under title.

  Jane Yolen's old MacDonald songbook / selected, edited, and

introduced by Jane Yolen ; musical arrangements by Adam Stemple ; illustrations

by Rosekrans Hoffman.—1st ed.

[96]p. ; col. ill. ; cm.

Includes index.

Summary : A collection of traditional animal songs accompanied by music.

ISBN 1-56397-281-6

1. Folk songs. 2. Children's songs. 3. Animals—Songs and music—

Juvenile literature. [1. Folk songs. 2. Animals—Songs and music.]

I. Yolen, Jane. II. Stemple, Adam. III. Hoffman, Rosekrans, ill.

IV. Title.

784.6—dc20   1994   CIP

Library of Congress Catalog Card Number 93-73303

First edition, 1994

Book designed by Joy Chu

The text of this book is set in 15-point Cochin; the song lyrics are set in 13-point Cochin.

The illustrations are colored inks.

Distributed by St. Martin's Press

10 9 8 7 6 5 4 3 2 1

For Jane Dyer,

a familiar face

at the Funny Farm

—J.Y.

For Helen Wohlberg

and Morris Kirchoff

—R.H.

Contents

Singing Old MacDonald

OLD MACDONALD, that consummate folk song farmer, has an infinitely expandable barnyard. Depending upon how much fun the young singers are having, he can own cows, horses, hens, ducks, dogs, cats, chicks, and more. I have been in groups that have even tried giving old Farmer M. a range of exotic animals—elephants, stoats, giraffes, toads. We had no idea how these beasts sounded. So of course we made them up, to the delight of all.

Most of the songs in this book were originally meant for adults to sing, but quite naturally children adopted them all. Songs that began as love songs, work songs, game songs, minstrel show songs, as fiddle tunes and banjo tunes—if the children came to love them, they *became* children's songs.

Some of the songs herein have complicated lineages—based on rhymes, historical references, or parts of farm language, for example—and some were composed by popular musicians. But all have that certain something that appeals to the children. Most of them are songs I heard as a child, either from my own parents (my father played the ukulele and guitar, my mother the piano), at school, or at camp. I passed them on to my own children. I expect one day to hear the next generation singing the "old" songs with gusto: "Old MacDonald," "Old Blue," "Old Gray Mare," "The Old Cow Died," "The Old Woman and Her Pig," and the rest.

My son Adam Stemple has put the songs into simple piano arrangements with guitar chords as well. So now these songs can travel on, from our family to yours, not the old way by mouth-to-ear resuscitation, but on the pages of this colorful book.

As one nursery rhyme has it:

"Then let us sing, merrily,
    merrily now,
We'll live on the custards
    that come from the cow."

—**J**ane Yolen

Old MacDonald Had a Farm

A traditional English/American song, this cumulative ditty can be expanded for any number of animals, from the true barnyard crew to the rare and exotic. Anyone know what kind of sound a hedgehog makes? Or a kangaroo?

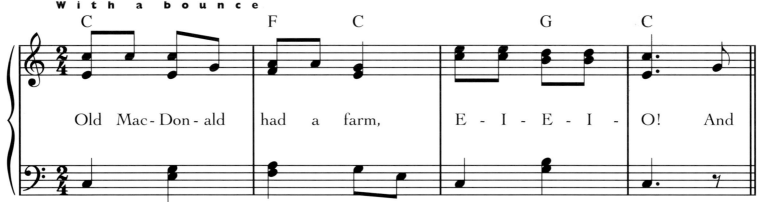

Old Mac-Don-ald had a farm, E - I - E - I - O! And

on this farm he had { 1. a dog, 2. some ducks } E - I - E - I - O! With a

bow-wow here, And a

bow-wow there. Here a

bow, there a wow,

quack-quack

quack-quack

quack, quack,

Ev-'ry-where a bow-wow,

quack-quack

Old Mac-Don-ald had a farm, E - I - E - I - O! (And)

3. And on this farm he had some horses,
E-I-E-I-O!
With a neigh-neigh here, . . . etc.

4. And on this farm he had some chicks,
E-I-E-I-O!
With a chick-chick here, . . . etc.

9

Have a Little Dog

In Texas there are hundreds of songs just about dogs. This popular one is often called "Toll-A-Winker." "Going to tongue" is the kind of barking a hunting hound utters when it sights its prey.

In a jolly manner

1. Have a lit-tle dog and his name is Don,

Continued

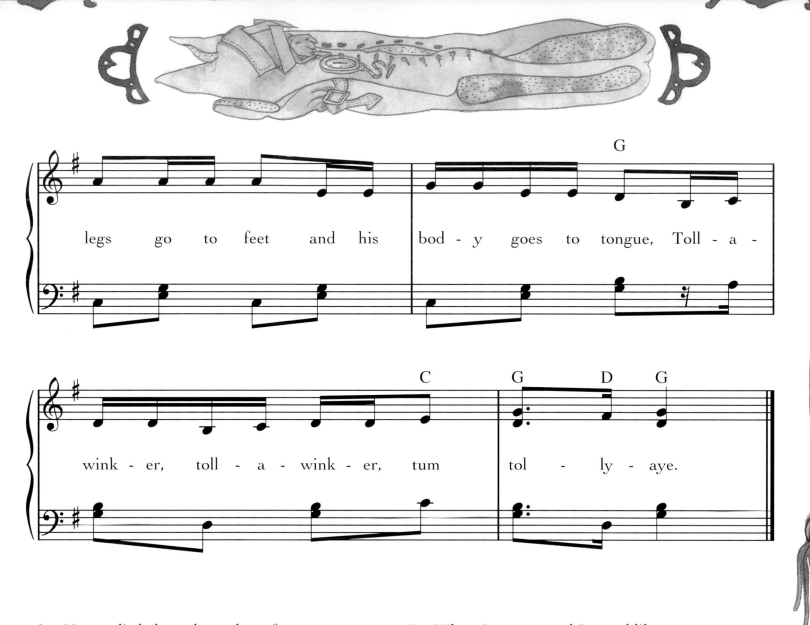

2. Have a little box about three feet square,
   (whistle)
   Have a little box about three feet square,
   When I go to travel I put him in there,
   Toll-a-winker, toll-a-winker, tum tolly-aye.

3. When I go to travel I travel like an ox,
   (whistle two times)
   And in my vest pocket I carry that box, . . . etc.

Bow-Wow-Wow

The words to this song come from a book published in 1760 by John Newbery—*Mother Goose's Melody*. Tom Tinker refers to an itinerant mender of pots and pans, a tinker. Often the tinkers were gypsies.

Simply

D   G(D bass)   D

Bow - wow - wow,   Whose dog art thou?

A(C♯ bass)   Bm   G(B bass)   D(A bass) A   D

Lit - tle Tom - my Tink - er's dog,   Bow - wow - wow.

Where, Oh Where Has My Little Dog Gone?

An anonymous American college song popular at the turn of the century, this classic was brought back again as a pop song in the 1950s. "Grog" is a kind of alcoholic drink, usually made with rum.

Wistfully

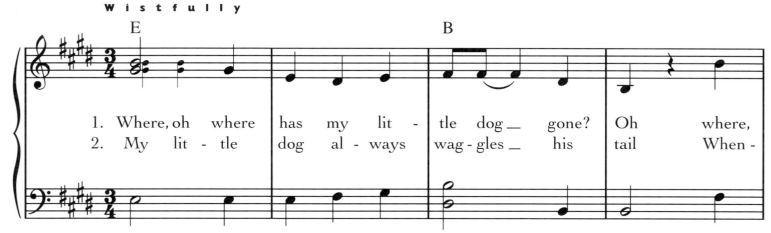

1. Where, oh where has my lit - tle dog ___ gone? Oh where,
2. My lit - tle dog al - ways wag - gles ___ his tail When -

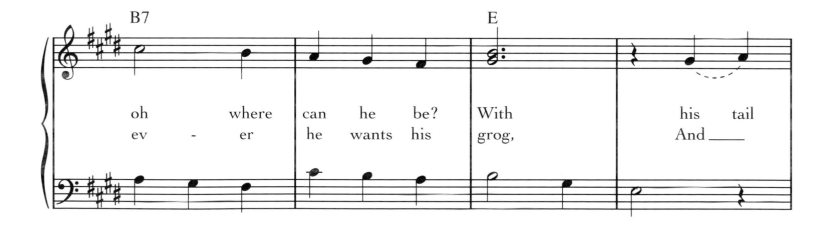

oh where can he be? With his tail
ev - er he wants his grog, And ___

15

ld Dog Tray

Stephen Foster, the most popular nineteenth century composer in America, wrote this in memory of a setter he once owned. In the first eighteen months after it was published, it sold 125,000 copies in sheet music.

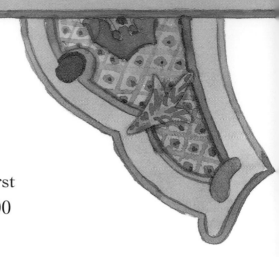

on the vil-lage green, A - sport-ing with my old dog, Tray.

Old dog Tray's ev - er faith - ful. Grief can-not drive him a -

Continued

17

Old Blue

A popular Southern song, this originated in the Mississippi Valley where there are many versions of both the words and the tune.

Drivingly

1. I had a dog and his name was Blue.
I had — a dog and his name was Blue.
I had — a dog and his name was Blue.
Bet you five dol-lars he's a good dog, —

Continued

19

2. When old Blue was a-diggin' around
   Never 'llowed a possum for to touch the ground.

3. When old Blue died, he died so hard,
   Shook the ground in my backyard.

4. Dug his grave with a silver spade
   And lowered him down with a golden chain.

5. Lowered him down with a golden chain,
   Ev'ry link I did call his name.

Three Little Kittens

ften attributed to Eliza Follen because she published it in her book *New Nursery Songs for All Good Children* in 1843, this song is really a traditional rhyme.

Plaintively

1. Three lit - tle kit - tens, they lost their mit - tens, And they be - gan __ to cry, "Oh, Moth - er, dear, __ we sad - ly fear, __ Our

2. Three lit - tle kit - tens, they found their mit - tens, And they be - gan __ to cry, "Oh, Moth - er, dear, __ see here, see here, __ Our

The Cat Came Back

Written by Harry S. Miller for a minstrel show just before the turn of the century, this song had a French ancestor, "Le Chat de Mère Michelle."

Jauntily

1.   Old   Mis - ter John - son   had   troub - les of his own, He   had   a yel-low   cat   that
2.   The man a-round the cor - ner swore he'd   kill   the cat on sight. He   load-ed up his shot-gun with

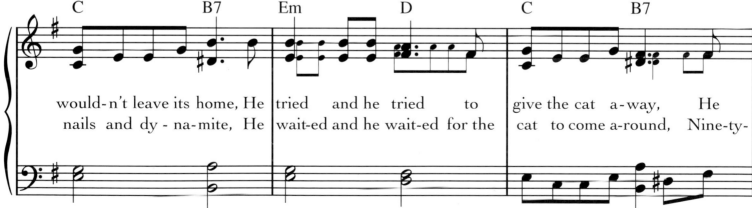

would-n't leave its home, He   tried   and he tried   to   give the cat a-way,   He
nails   and dy - na-mite, He   wait-ed and he wait-ed for the   cat   to come a-round,   Nine-ty-

24

Three Little Piggies

This traditional American folk song has a moral: a very conservative moral at that.

Straightforwardly

1. Once was a sow who had three lit-tle pig-gies; Three lit-
2. One____ day one of those three lit-tle pig-gies To the

tle pig-gies had she. And the old sow ___
oth - er two pig-gies said he, "Why ___

26

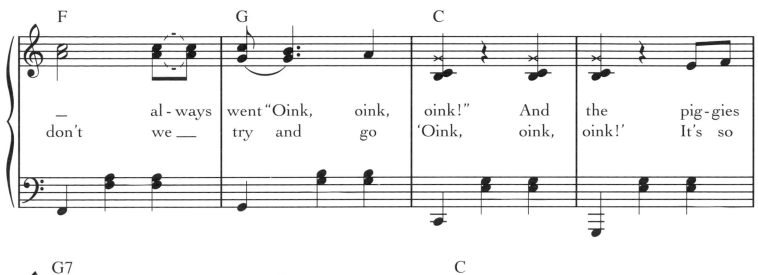

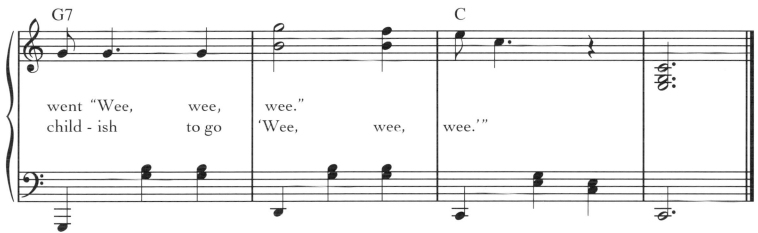

F

G

C

_ al - ways went "Oink, oink, oink!" And the pig-gies
don't we __ try and go 'Oink, oink, oink!' It's so

G7

C

went "Wee, wee, wee."
child - ish to go 'Wee, wee, wee.'"

3. Those little piggies grew skinny and lean,
   Skinny they well might be.
   For they all tried to go "Oink, oink, oink,"
   And could only go "Wee, wee, wee."

4. Those little piggies they upped and they died,
   A very sad sight to see.
   So don't you try and go "Oink, oink, oink,"
   When you ought to go "Wee, wee, wee."

Sow Got the Measles

A popular American folk song found all over the States, this tune originally traveled from Ireland to New England.

1. How do you think I be-gan in this world? I got me a sow and
2. What do you think I made of her_ hide? The very best sad-dle you

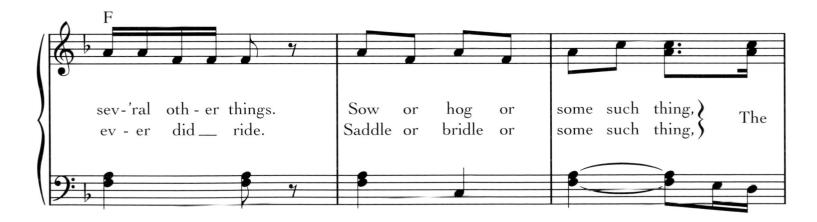

sev-'ral oth-er things.
ev-er did_ ride.

Sow or hog or
Saddle or bridle or

some such thing, } The
some such thing, }

C7   **F**

sow   got   the   mea - sles   and   she   died   in   the   spring.

3. What do you think I made of her nose?
   The very best thimble that ever sewed clothes.
   Thimble or needle or some such thing,
   The sow got the measles and she died in the spring.

4. What do you think I made of her feet?
   The very best pickles you ever did eat.
   Pickles or glue or some such thing,
   The sow got the measles and she died in the spring.

29

The Little Pig

This is a Texas version of a popular barnyard song. For another way of singing it, see "The Old Woman and Her Pig."

1. There was an old wom-an and she had a lit-tle pig, — Oink, oink,
2. That lit-tle pig — did a heap — of — harm, —

oink. There was an old wom-an and she had a lit-tle pig, It
That lit-tle pig — did a heap — of — harm, A -

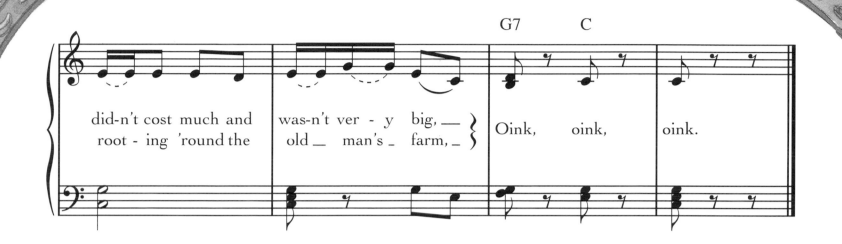

did-n't cost much and
root - ing 'round the

was-n't ver - y big, —
old — man's — farm, —

Oink, oink, oink.

3. The little pig died for want of breath, . . . etc.
   Now wasn't that an awful death! . . . etc.

4. The little old woman, she sobbed and she sighed, . . . etc.
   Then she lay right down and died, . . . etc.

5. The old man died for want of grief, . . . etc.
   Wasn't that a great relief! . . . etc.

6. There they lay, all one, two, three, . . . etc.
   The man, the woman, and the little pig-gie, . . . etc.

7. There they lay all on the shelf, . . . etc.
   If you want any more, you can sing it yourself, . . . etc.

31

The Old Woman and Her Pig

A Southern banjo tune, this song shares some lines with "The Little Pig," but this one is a much nicer piggie for all that.

With a bounce

1. There was an old wom-an and she had a lit-tle pig,
old wom-an kept ____ the pig-gie in the barn,
Go tell my true love.

33

Continued

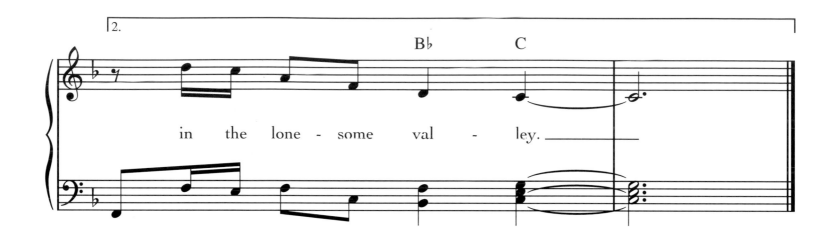

B♭   C

in the lone - some val - ley. _____

3. Well, the little pig, he fed on clover,
   And when he died, he died all over.

4. The old woman, she died of grief,
   And wasn't that a great relief.

Lambs to Sell

Long before there were radio and television commercials, people sold their wares on street corners and at outdoor markets by singing out songs or cries. Each street vendor had his or her own special way of calling, a kind of "trademark."

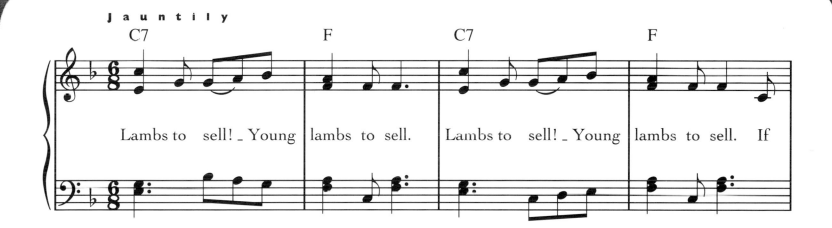

Jauntily

Lambs to sell! _ Young lambs to sell. Lambs to sell! _ Young lambs to sell. If

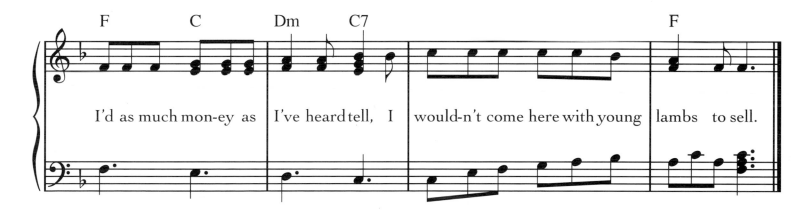

I'd as much mon-ey as I've heard tell, I would-n't come here with young lambs to sell.

35

Sheep Shearing

This song is almost 250 years old. Still popular among British country folk, it celebrates a part of farming that is as present today in England and Scotland as it was a hundred years ago.

With a lilt

1. How de - light-ful to see   In the eve - nings in spring, The __
2. The sixth month of the year, In the month call - éd June, When the

sheep go - ing home to the fold.   The __ mas - ter does sing As he
weath-er's too hot to be borne,   The __ mas - ter doth say As he

36

3. Now as for those sheep,
   They're delightful to see,
   They're a blessing to man on his farm.
   For their flesh it is good,
   It's the best of all food.
   And the wool it will clothe us up warm.
   And the wool it will clothe us up warm.

4. Now the sheep they're all shorn,
   And the wool carried home.
   Here's a health to our master and flock.
   And if we should stay
   Till the last goes away,
   I'm afraid 'twill be past twelve o'clock.
   I'm afraid 'twill be past twelve o'clock.

I Wish I Had the Shepherd's Lamb

The chorus of this Irish children's song is partly in Gaelic. It means: "And O! I call you, I call you. You are my heart's love without deceit, and you are your mother's little pet."

Sweetly

1. I ___ wish I had the shep-herd's lamb, The shep-herd's lamb, the shep-herd's lamb. I

wish I had the shep-herd's lamb And Ka - tie com - ing af - ter *(chorus)* Iss

38

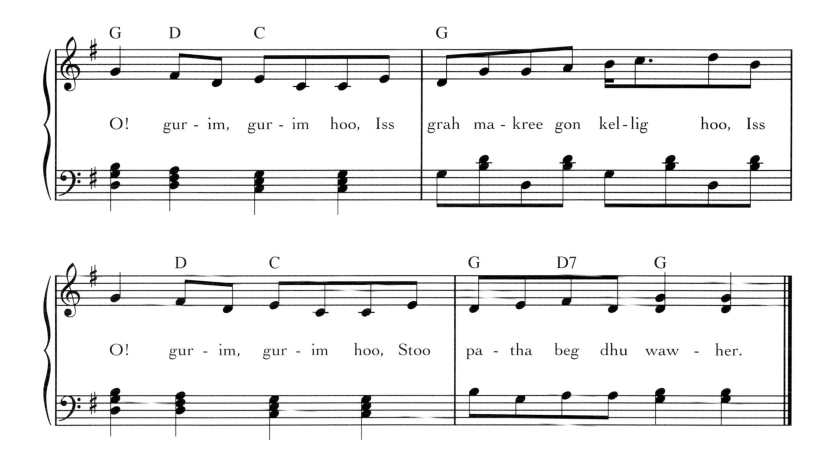

2. I wish I had the yellow cow,
   The yellow cow, the yellow cow.
   I wish I had the yellow cow
   And welcome from my darling.
   (chorus)

3. I wish I had a herd of kine,
   A herd of kine, a herd of kine.
   I wish I had a herd of kine,
   And Katie from her father.
   (chorus)

Black Sheep, Black Sheep

Using some of the same words as the poignant lullaby "All the Pretty Little Horses," this song was sung by slave mothers in the South.

Poignantly

E   E7   A   E   E6

Black sheep, black sheep, where's your lamb? 'Way down in the

B7   E   (E bass) E   A   E6   E   E6

val - ley. _____ Bees and the but-ter-flies pick-ing out its eyes,

Poor lit-tle thing cry-in' "Mam - my." Black sheep, black sheep,

where's your lamb? 'Way down in the val - ley.

The Darby Ram

Though this seems like a typical brag song, it is also part of an old British winter ritual, "The Darby Tup," performed by five or six mummers going house to house at Christmastime. Rams were associated for centuries with the English town of Derby (pronounced Darby). When the song crossed the ocean to America, it was so popular, it became George Washington's favorite song.

With gusto

G   G(F♯ bass)   Em   G   C   D

1. As   I   was going   to   Dar - by, 'Twas on a mar - ket

day,   I   saw   the   big - gest   ram,   sir,   That

ev - er was fed   on   hay.   That   ev - er was fed   on   hay.

2. That ram was fat behind, sir,
   That ram was fat before.
   It measured six yards 'round, sir,
   And I think it was no more.
   And I think it was no more.

3. The horns upon its head, sir,
   As high as a man can reach.
   And there they built a pulpit,
   The Quakers for to preach, sir,
   The Quakers for to preach.

4. The hair upon its belly,
   It reached to the ground
   And sold in Darby town, sir,
   For forty-seven pound.
   For forty-seven pound.

5. Indeed, sir, and it's true, sir,
   I've never been known to lie.
   And if you'd been to Darby,
   You'd seen it as well as I, sir,
   You'd seen it as well as I.

43

Gray Goose

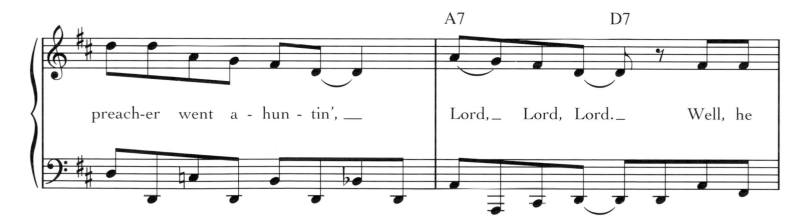

In Africa, leader and chorus songs are still very popular. When Africans were brought to America to work as slaves, they carried pieces of their culture with them. This song from the prisons of the South, with its leader-chorus pattern, reminds us of that rough passage.

With enthusiasm

1. It was one Sun-day morn-ing, — Lord, Lord, Lord, The

preach-er went a-hun-tin', — Lord,— Lord, Lord.— Well, he

car-ried 'long his shot-gun, . Lord, Lord, Lord, He car-ried 'long his shot-gun, .

1. A7 D7 2. A7 D7

Lord, _ Lord, Lord. 2. And a- Lord, _ Lord, Lord.

Continued

2. And along come the gray goose,
Lord, Lord, Lord,
Along come the gray goose,
Lord, Lord, Lord.
Well, the gun went off, baloom,
Lord, Lord, Lord,
And down come the gray goose,
Lord, Lord, Lord.

3. He was six weeks a-fallin',
Lord, Lord, Lord,
We was six weeks a-haulin',
Lord, Lord, Lord.
Then your wife and my wife,
Lord, Lord, Lord,
They had a feather-pickin',
Lord, Lord, Lord.

4. Then they put him in the oven,
Lord, Lord, Lord,
But the oven wouldn't cook him,
Lord, Lord, Lord.
They put him on the table,
Lord, Lord, Lord,
The knife wouldn't cut him,
Lord, Lord, Lord.

5. They took him to the sawmill,
Lord, Lord, Lord,
He broke the saw's teeth out,
Lord, Lord, Lord.
They flung him to the sky,
Lord, Lord, Lord,
Well, they flung him to the sky,
Lord, Lord, Lord.

6. And the last time I seed him,
Lord, Lord, Lord,
He was flying 'cross the sky,
Lord, Lord, Lord.
With a long string of goslings,
Lord, Lord, Lord,
With a long string of goslings,
Lord, Lord, Lord.

7. And they all goin' quink-quank,
Lord, Lord, Lord,
And they all goin' quink-quank,
Lord, Lord, Lord.
They all goin' quink-quank,
Lord, Lord, Lord,
They all goin' quink-quank,
Lord, Lord, Lord.

Why Shouldn't My Goose?

This anonymous four-part round is several centuries old. It comes from England.

Straightforwardly

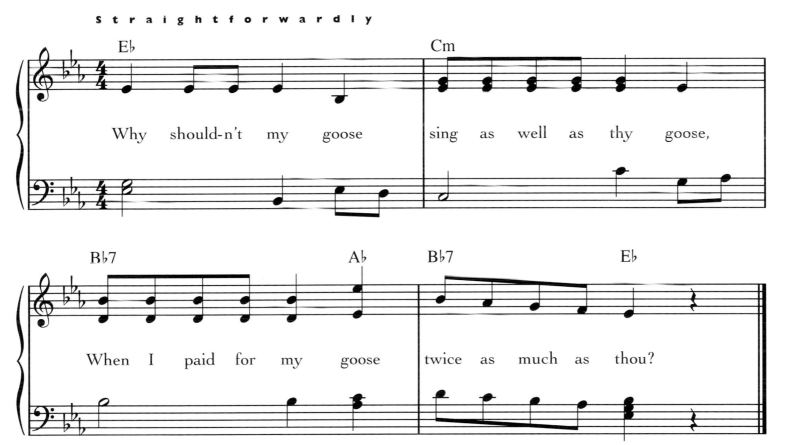

Why should-n't my goose sing as well as thy goose,

When I paid for my goose twice as much as thou?

Go Tell Aunt Rhody

Aunt Rhody has a lot of different names, depending where this is sung. She is Aunt Patsy in the South, Aunt Nancy in the West, and even Aunt Dinah, Aunt Tildy, and Aunt Tabby.

With mock sadness

1. Go tell Aunt Rho - dy,
one she'd been sav - ing, The

Go tell Aunt Rho - dy,
one she'd been sav - ing, The

Go tell Aunt Rho - dy The
one she'd been sav - ing To

old gray goose is __ dead. 2. The

make a feath-er __ bed.

48

3. The goslings are crying,
   The goslings are crying,
   The goslings are crying
   Because their ma is dead.

4. She died in the millpond,
   She died in the millpond,
   She died in the millpond
   A-standing on her head.

5. So go tell Aunt Rhody,
   Go tell Aunt Rhody,
   Go tell Aunt Rhody
   The old gray goose is dead.

OLD
GRAY
GOOSE
BORN   DIED

Ducks in the Millpond

A Virginia fiddle tune, this song has a number of other verses that have nothing to do with ducks at all.

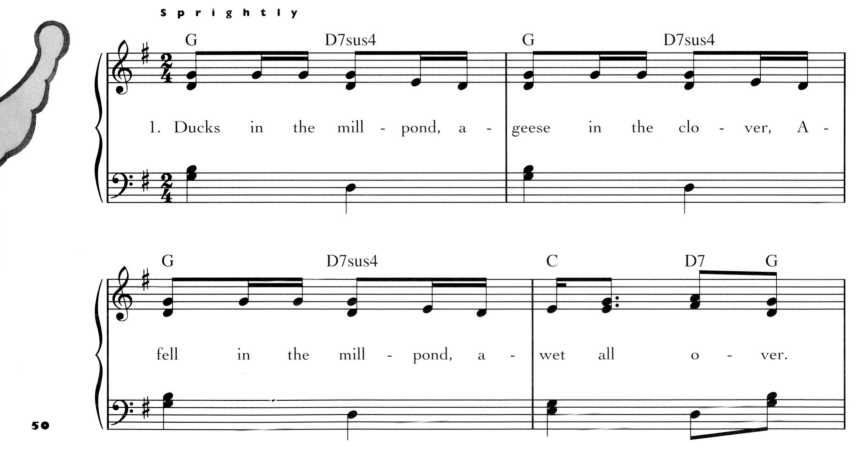

Sprightly

1. Ducks in the mill - pond, a - geese in the clo - ver, A -
fell in the mill - pond, a - wet all o - ver.

2. Ducks in the millpond, a-geese in the clover,
   Jumped in the bed, and the bed turned over.

3. Ducks in the millpond, a-geese in the ocean,
   A-hug them pretty girls if I take a notion.

Mistress Bond

Throughout England and America the country folk call their farm animals to feed with special cries. In England "Dilly, dilly . . ." calls the ducks. Before this was a song, it was a popular British nursery rhyme.

Innocently

1. Oh, what have you got there for din - ner, Mis-tress Bond? There's
2. I have been to the ducks that swim in the pond, But

beef in the lar - der and ducks in the pond. Cry } dil-ly, dil-ly, dil-ly, dil-ly,
I found that they won't be killed, Mis-tress Bond. I cried }

come and be killed, For you must be stuffed and my cus - tom-ers filled.

Be Kind to Your Web-footed Friends

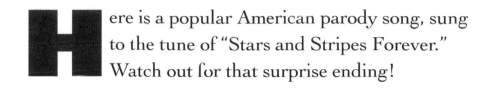ere is a popular American parody song, sung to the tune of "Stars and Stripes Forever." Watch out for that surprise ending!

John Philip Sousa

Have fun!

Be kind to your web - foot - ed friends, For a

duck may be some - bod-y's moth - er. Be kind to the den-i-zens of the

The Old Gray Hen

This old French song is called "La Poulette Grise," and additional verses sing about different-colored hens.

Flowingly

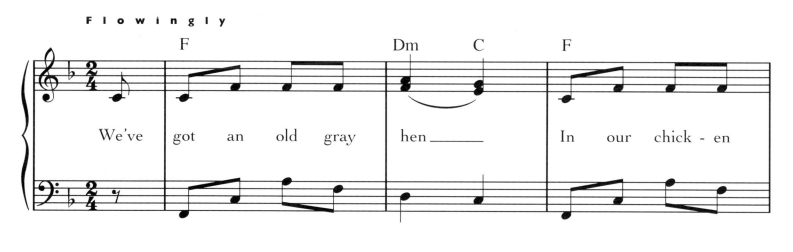

We've got an old gray hen ____ In our chick - en

pen, ____ She will lay a ver - y pret - ty egg For a { girl / boy } by the

name of { Jen- ny. / Mi - chael. | She will lay   a | ver-y pret-ty egg | For a { girl / boy if { she / he

goes to sleep, | Sleep, my { girl, / boy, | sleep. _____

I Love My Rooster

This cumulative song consists of American words grafted onto the classic Scottish tune "The Campbells Are Coming."

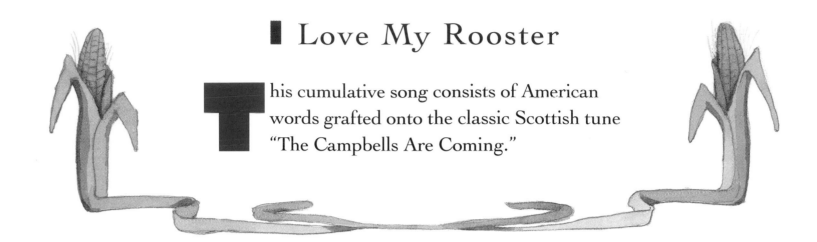

With joy

I love — my roost - er, my roost - er loves me; I

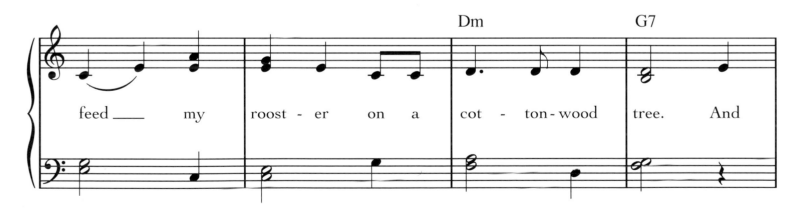

feed — my roost - er on a cot - ton-wood tree. And

The Chickens They Are Crowing

Originally a game song, related to "We're Marching Doen to Rauser's," this American folk song has many more verses linked to courting customs in the Appalachians.

Plaintively

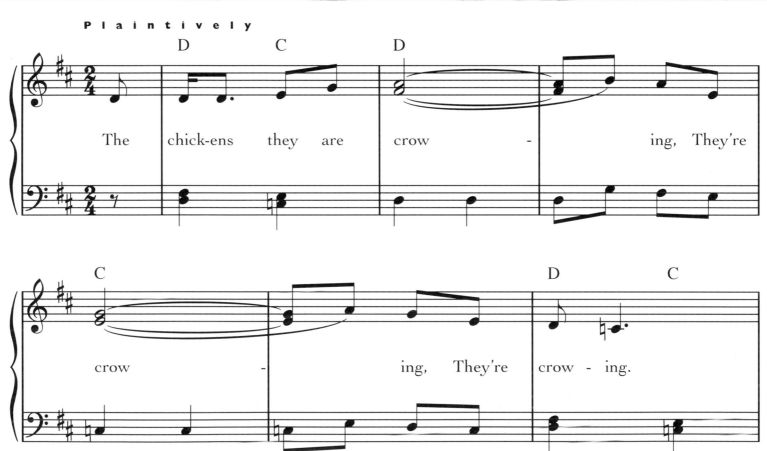

The chick-ens they are crow - ing, They're crow - ing, They're crow - ing.

The chick-ens they are crow-ing, For it is 'most day-light.

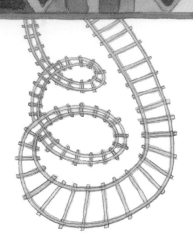
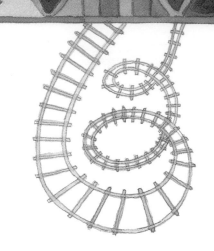

My Old Hen

The nursery rhyme ancestor of this song begins "Hickety, pickety, my black hen . . ." It was collected by Father Goose, as James O. Halliwell-Phillips was called, in the mid-nineteenth century. The music has its own history. It is an American fiddle tune.

My old hen's a good old hen, She lays eggs for the rail - road men.

Some-times one, some-times two, Some-times e-nough for the whole dern crew.

E	A	E	B	E	A	E	B

Cluck, old hen, cluck, I tell you, Cluck, old hen, or I'm gon-na sell you.

E	A	E	B	E	A	B7	E

Cluck, old hen, cluck, I say, Cluck, old hen, or I'll give you a-way.

Turkey in the Straw

A popular American fiddle tune, this was first sung in New York City in 1834. Today it is more often performed at square dances.

1. As __ I was a-go-ing on __ down the road With a ti - red team . and a

heav-y load, I ___ cracked my __ whip __ and the lead-er sprung; I ___

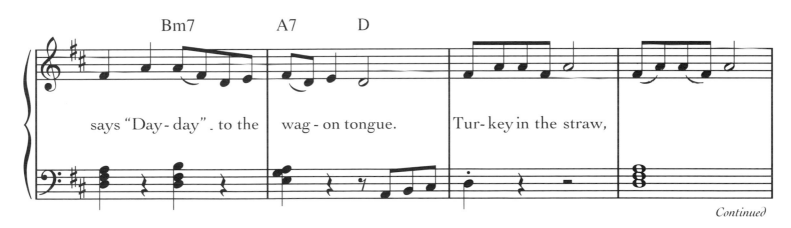

says "Day - day" . to the wag - on tongue. Tur- key in the straw,

65

Continued

G   D

Tur-key in the hay,   Roll 'em up and twist 'em up a-

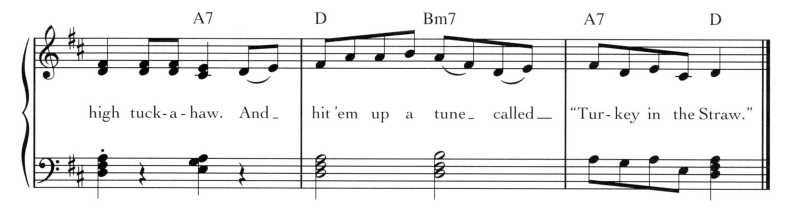

A7   D   Bm7   A7   D

high tuck-a-haw. And   hit 'em up a tune called "Tur-key in the Straw."

2.   Oh, I went out to milk but I didn't know how,
     I milked a goat instead of a cow.
     A monkey sitting on a pile of straw,
     A-winking his eye at his mother-in-law. . . . etc.

3.   Came to the river and I couldn't get across,
     So I paid five dollars for an old blind horse.
     Well, he wouldn't go ahead and he wouldn't stand still,
     So he went up and down like an old sawmill. . . . etc.

The Turkey

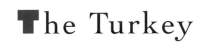

In Hungarian this song is called "Debreczenbe Kéne Menni." The great composer Béla Bartók used this song as the basis for one of his pieces for the piano.

Plainly

C   Am   F   C

This old road is hard and bump - y,   Our new tur-key's wild and jump - y.

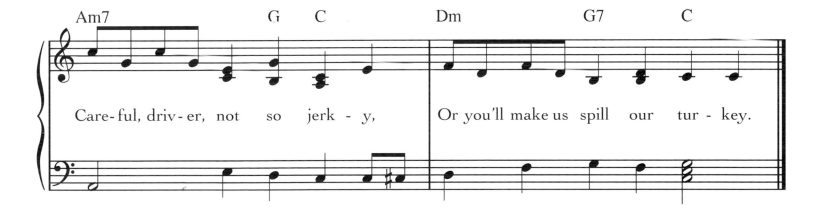

Am7   G   C   Dm   G7   C

Care-ful, driv - er, not so jerk - y,   Or you'll make us spill our tur - key.

67

Counting the Goats

This is a tongue twister in Welsh, a popular singing game among Welsh farmhands.

Sturdily

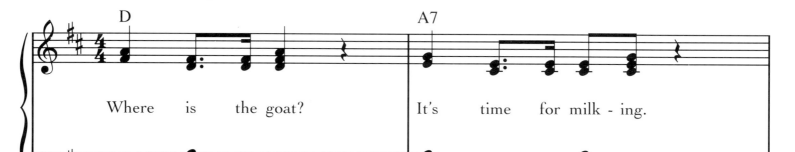

Where is the goat? It's time for milk - ing.

Off a-mong the crag-gy rocks The old goat is wan-d'ring. Goat white, white, white,

Bill Grogan's Goat

A popular camp song, this tune first found favor on American music hall stages. If there ever was a real Bill Grogan — or his goat — we will never know.

G   C

1. Bill Gro-gan's goat Was feel-ing fine, Ate three red

D   G

shirts From off the line.

2. Bill grabbed that goat
   By the wool of his back,
   And tied him to
   The railroad track.

3. That goat he bucked
   With might and main,
   As round the curve
   Came a passenger train.

4. That goat he bucked
   With might and main,
   Coughed up those shirts
   And flagged the train.

71

Mary Had a William Goat

This punning tavern song is sung to the tune of that old favorite "Mary Had a Little Lamb."

Jauntily

1. Mar - y had a Wil - liam goat,

Wil - liam goat, Wil - liam goat, Mar - y had a

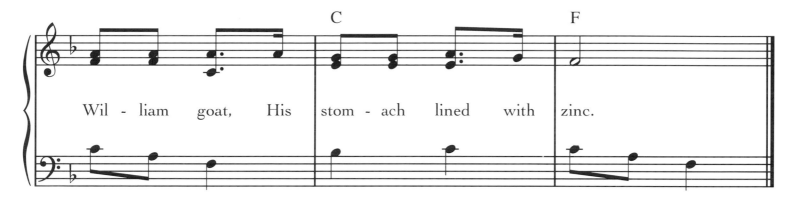

Wil - liam goat, His stom - ach lined with zinc.

2. He followed her to school one day,
   School one day, school one day,
   He followed her to school one day
   And drank a pot of ink.

3. One day he ate an oyster can,
   Oyster can, oyster can,
   One day he ate an oyster can
   And a clothesline full of shirts.

4. The shirts can do no harm inside,
   Harm inside, harm inside,
   The shirts can do no harm inside,
   But the oyster can.

73

The Little Black Bull

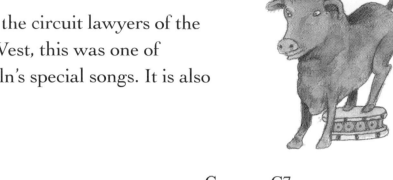

A favorite song of the circuit lawyers of the pre-Civil War West, this was one of Abraham Lincoln's special songs. It is also called "Hoosen Johnny."

Simply

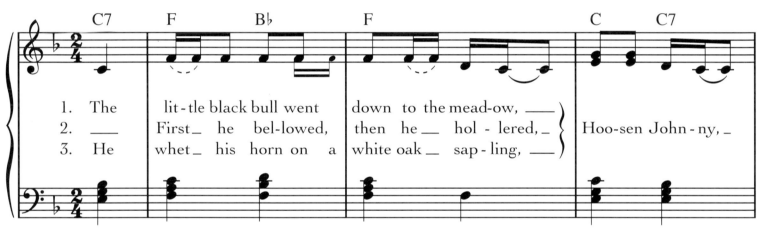

C7 F Bb F C C7

1. The lit-tle black bull went down to the mead-ow, ___ } Hoo-sen John-ny, ___
2. ___ First ___ he bel-lowed, then he ___ hol-lered, ___ }
3. He whet ___ his horn on a white oak ___ sap-ling, ___ }

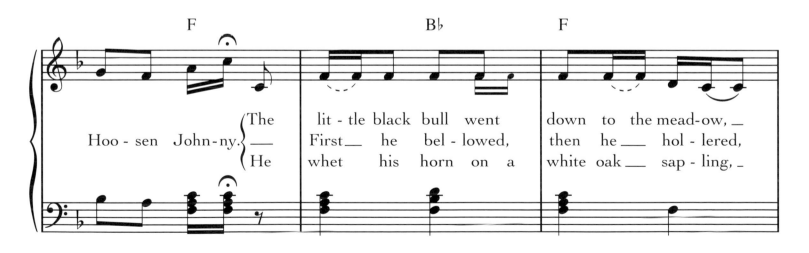

F Bb F

Hoo-sen John-ny. { The lit-tle black bull went down to the mead-ow, ___
                  { He whet his horn on a ... First ___ he bel-lowed, then he ___ hol-lered,
                                                white oak ___ sap-ling, ___

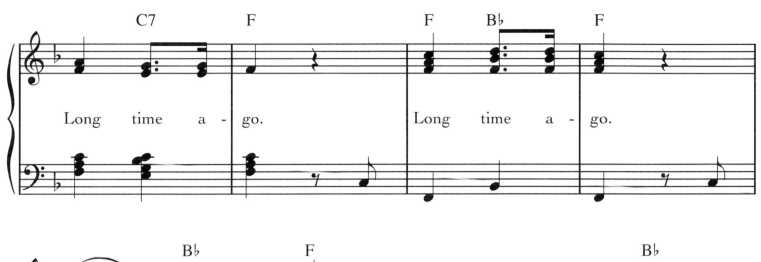

Long time a - go. Long time a - go.

Long ___ time a - go. The lit - tle black bull went

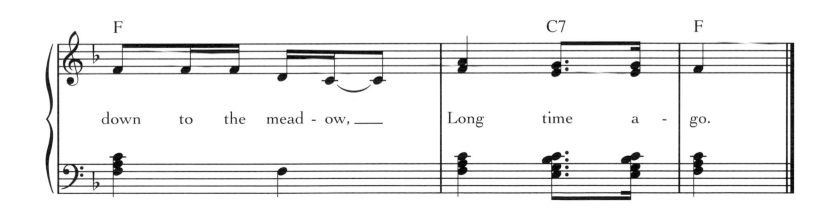

down to the mead - ow, ___ Long time a - go.

The Cow

This pleasant British song actually holds out a very good warning. Hemlock is a poisonous weed of the carrot family, while the cowslip—or English primrose—is a flower found in meadows and along the hedgerows and which, according to herbalries, has a soothing and quieting effect.

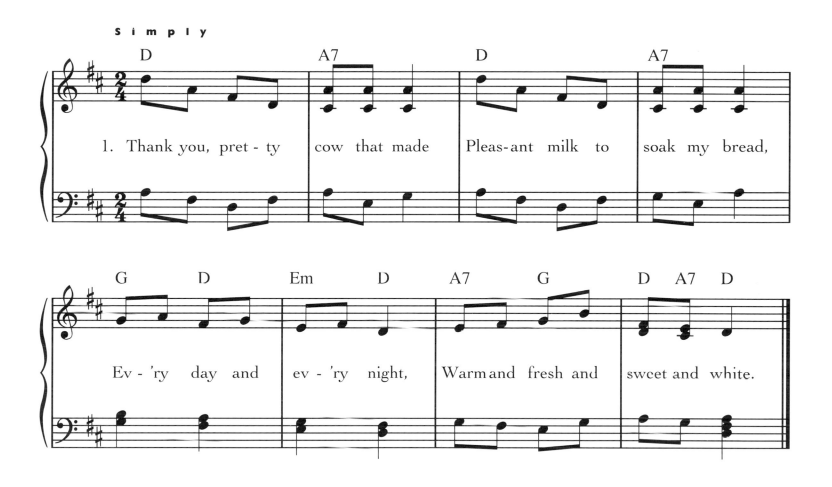

2. Do not chew the hemlock rank,
    Growing on the weedy bank;
    But the yellow cowslips eat.
    They will make your milk so sweet.

3. Where the purple violet grows,
    Where the bubbling water flows,
    Where the grass is fresh and fine,
    Pretty cow, go there and dine.

77

The Old Cow Died

A leader and chorus song from the Southern mountains, this is closely related to "Hey, Little Boy."

With mock sadness

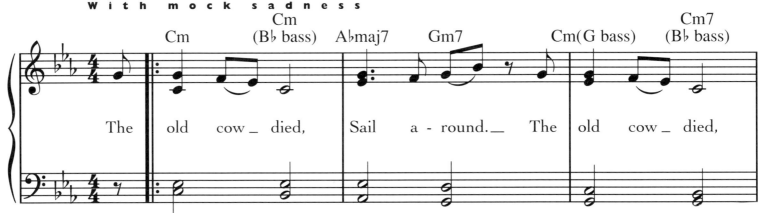

The old cow _ died, Sail a - round._ The old cow _ died,

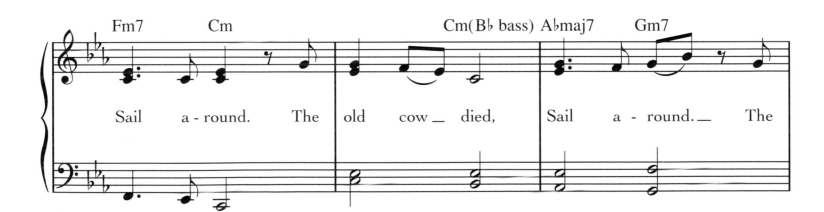

Sail a - round. The old cow _ died, Sail a - round._ The

2. Did you find what ailed her?
   Yes, ma'am.
   Did she die of the cholera?
   Yes, ma'am.

3. Did the buzzards come then?
   Yes, ma'am.
   Did the buzzards eat her?
   Yes, ma'am.

4. Did they sail high?
   Yes, ma'am.
   Did they sail low?
   Yes, ma'am.

Shoe the Old Horse

There are a number of versions to this old nursery rhyme. It is a lap game that is popular on both sides of the Atlantic. On the words "shoe the old horse" the child's left foot gets a pat. Say "shoe the old mare," and the right foot gets a pat. Then the shoes and socks are taken off in rhythm to the rest of the song.

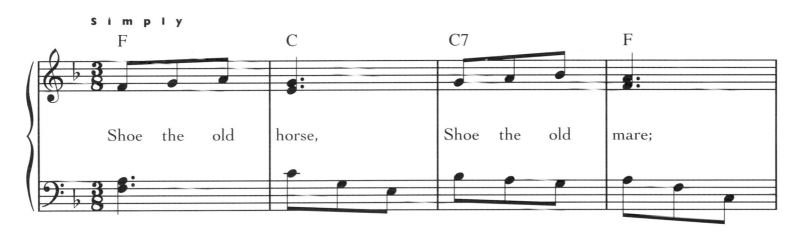

Simply

F — Shoe the old horse,
C — Shoe the old mare;
C7 — F —

F#dim — Let lit - tle colt go
Gm6 — C — bare,___ bare,
C7 — F — bare.

My Horses Ain't Hungry

There is a much longer version of this song—a love song in which the young man tells his true love that he is leaving because her family doesn't want a poor suitor. This version is from Tennessee, but others have been found throughout the Appalachian Mountain communities.

Plaintively

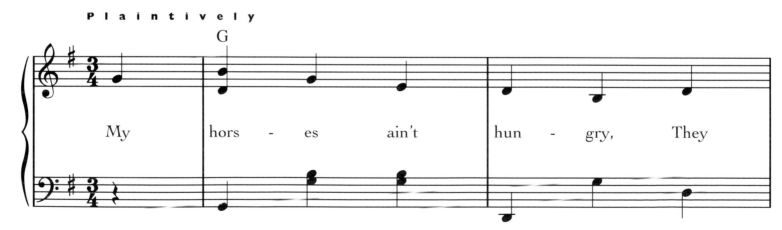

My   hors - es   ain't   hun - gry,   They

won't   eat   your   hay.   So   I'll   get   on   my

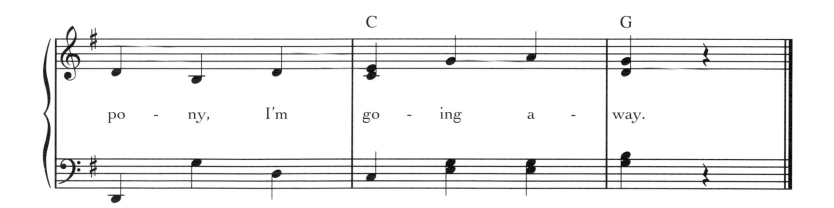

po - ny,   I'm   go - ing   a - way.

The Old Gray Mare

The tune of this American song, popular in schools and camps, is the Negro spiritual "The Old Gray Mare Came Tearin' Out of the Wilderness."

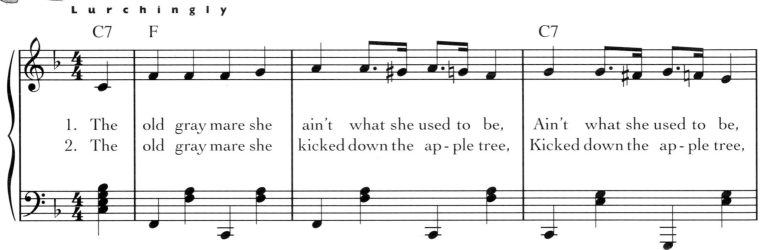

Lurchingly

C7   F   C7

1. The old gray mare she ain't what she used to be, Ain't what she used to be,
2. The old gray mare she kicked down the ap-ple tree, Kicked down the ap-ple tree,

F

Ain't what she used to be. The old gray mare she ain't what she used to be
Kicked down the ap-ple tree. The old gray mare she kicked down the ap-ple tree,

Hey, Little Boy

Sung by a leader and chorus, this is a Southern mountain play-party song. See how it is similar to "The Old Cow Died."

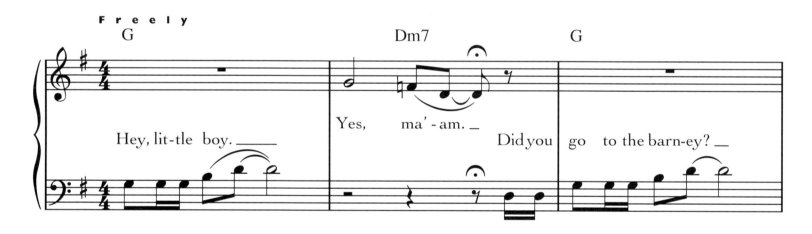

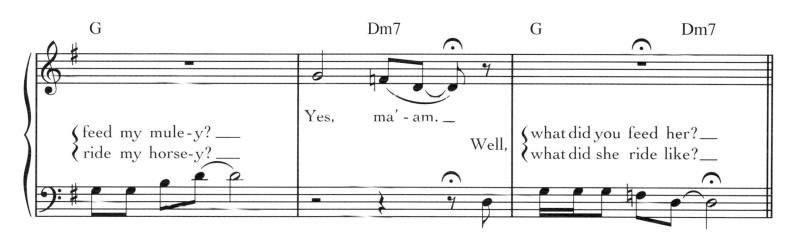

G   Dm7   G   Dm7

{ feed my mule-y? ___
{ ride my horse-y? ___

Yes,   ma' - am. ___

Well,

{ what did you feed her? ___
{ what did she ride like? ___

1.

G   Dm7   G

Fed her oats _ and bar-ley, _

Fed her oats _ and bar-ley, _

Fed her oats _ and bar-ley, _

87

Continued

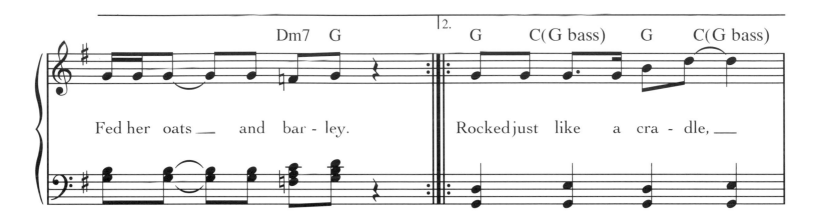

Fed her oats ___ and bar - ley.

Rocked just like a cra - dle, ___

Rocked just like a cra-dle, _

Rocked just like a cra-dle, _

Rocked just like a cra-dle. _

Donkeys and Carrots

Here is a four-part round from Belgium. The exact translation is "Donkeys love carrots, carrots don't love donkeys. Hee-haw, it is idiotic, but it is charming also."

With mock sadness

Don-keys are in love with car-rots, Car-rots aren't in love at all.

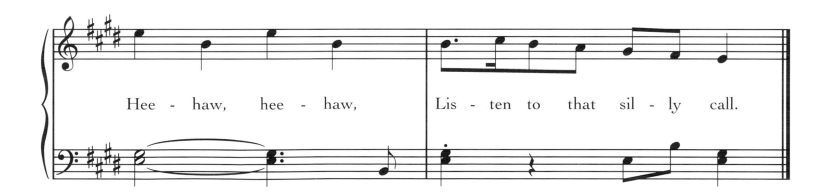

Hee - haw, hee - haw, Lis - ten to that sil - ly call.

89

Kicking Mule

Almost one hundred years old, this popular banjo tune is often played at Western square dances.

With spirit

1. My un - cle had   an old mule,   His   name was Si - mon Slick,   'Bove
   mule he is   a kick - er,   He's   got an i - ron back,   He

an - y - thing I ev - er did see Was   how that mule did kick.   Well,
head - ed off a Tex - as train And   kicked it off the track.

whoa there, mule, I tell you, Miz Li-za, you keep cool, I ain't got time to kiss you now, I'm

1.
fid - dl - ing with my mule. 2. That

2.
fid - dl - ing with my mule. ____

Mules

Sung to the Scottish tune of "Auld Lang Syne," this silly song makes a lot of sense if you take time to sort through the words.

With mock solemnity

On mules we find two legs be-hind, And two we find be - fore, We

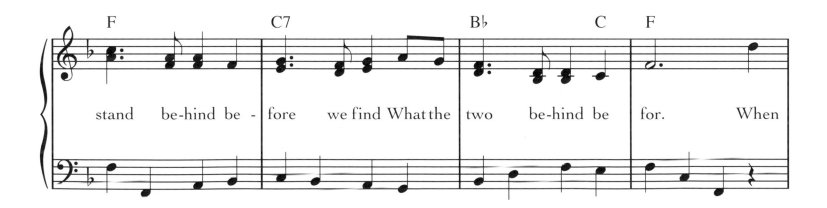

stand be-hind be - fore we find What the two be-hind be for. When

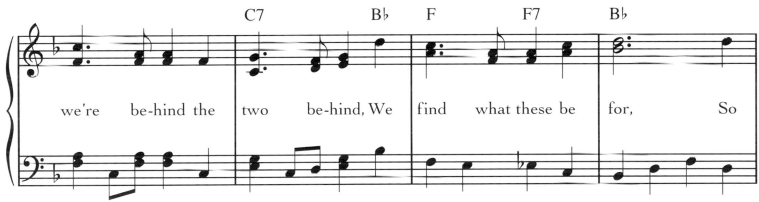

we're   be-hind the   two   be-hind, We   find   what these be   for,   So

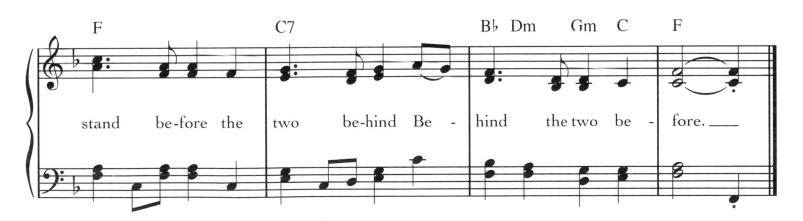

stand   be-fore the   two   be-hind Be - hind   the two be - fore. ___

Sweetly Sings the Donkey

A three-part round from England, this is heavy on sound effects and light on sense.

Gently — till the end

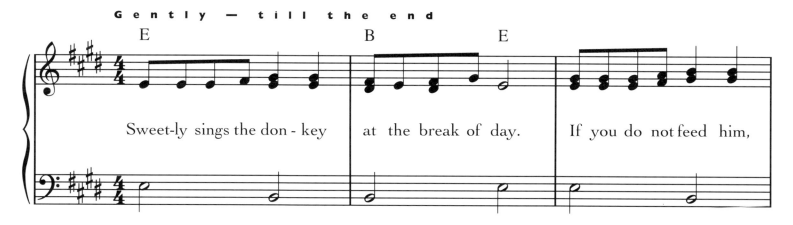

Sweet-ly sings the don-key | at the break of day. | If you do not feed him,

this is what he'll say: "Hee-haw, hee-haw, hee-haw, hee-haw, hee-haw."

JANE YOLEN is the celebrated author of more than one hundred and
thirty books for children, young adults, and adults. Her *Owl Moon*,
illustrated by John Schoenherr, won the 1988 Caldecott Medal. Among
her titles for Boyds Mills Press are *Jane Yolen's Mother Goose Songbook*, a
1993 International Reading Association/Children's Book Council
Children's Choice, *Sleep Rhymes Around the World*, and *Street Rhymes
Around the World*. She lives in Hatfield, Massachusetts.

ADAM STEMPLE, a composer as well as a guitarist and keyboard player,
is a member of Boiled in Lead, a Minneapolis-based band. His previous
books with his mother, Jane Yolen, are *Jane Yolen's Songs of Summer*,
*Jane Yolen's Mother Goose Songbook, The Lullaby Songbook, Hark! A
Christmas Sampler,* and *The Lap-Time Song & Play Book.* He lives in
Minneapolis, Minnesota.

ROSEKRANS HOFFMAN provided the illustrations for *Jane Yolen's Mother
Goose Songbook*, one of the more than twenty-five books she has
illustrated for children. Her paintings have been exhibited in several
museums, including the Whitney Museum and the Brooklyn Museum.
She lives in Lincoln, Nebraska.

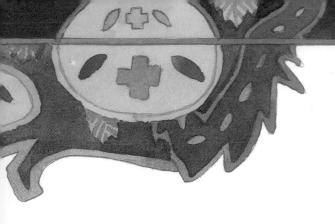
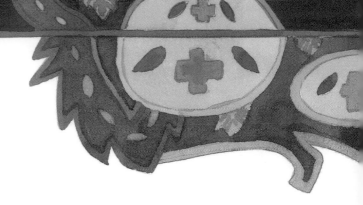

■$n\partial e x$

DATE			